PIGGY

piggy

Mireille Geus

TRANSLATED BY Nancy Forest-Flier

FRONT STREET
Asheville, North Carolina

Originally published under the title *Big*
by Lemniscaat b.v. Rotterdam, the Netherlands, 2005

Text copyright © 2005 by Mireille Geus
English translation copyright © 2008 by Nancy Forest-Flier
All rights reserved
Printed in China
Designed by Helen Robinson
First U.S. edition, 2008

This book was made possible by a grant from the Dutch Fund for Literature.

Library of Congress Cataloging-in-Publication Data
Geus, Mireille.
[Big. English]
Piggy / Mireille Geus ; [English translation by Nancy Forest-Flier]. — 1st U.S. ed.
p. cm.
Summary: Lizzie struggles to overcome the closed, internal world of autism
when a new girl moves into her neighborhood, befriends her,
then insists that Lizzie join her in seeking revenge on the boys who tease them.
ISBN 978-1-59078-636-9 (hardcover : alk. paper)
[1. Autism—Fiction. 2. Emotional problems—Fiction.
3. Friendship—Fiction. 4. Criminal investigation—Fiction.
5. Bullies—Fiction.] I. Forest, Nancy. II. Title.
PZ7.G335Pig 2008
[Fic]—dc22
2007048847

FRONT **STREET**
An Imprint of Boyds Mills Press, Inc.
815 Church Street
Honesdale, Pennsylvania 18431

PIGGY

NOW

Today I got a letter in the mail. I took it to the kitchen and tore it open. This is what it said:

Dear Dizzy,

How are you?

The people here wanted me to leave you alone for at least a year. So I did.

They said to me, if this is still on your mind after a year, you'll be allowed to write her a letter.

This is that letter.

What's still on my mind is that I really want to see you again.

How about coming to see me sometime? I'd really like that, blood sister.

There, I said it.

Anxiously waiting to see if you write back—or better, if you come see me.

Yours, Piggy.

I read the letter one more time and my hands started to shake.

My mother walked past with a cup of coffee. "What's that, honey?" she asked.

"A letter from Piggy," I said.

She brought her cup down hard on the table, then she took the letter from my trembling fingers. She read it and sighed, biting her lower lip.

"Is this never going to end?" said my mother.

We both sighed.

I've just had a lousy year, and this is the story of that lousy year.

The beginning of it, that is. Just the beginning, actually.

I've played it all over in my head a hundred times, everything that happened back then. Like a movie, or something on TV. That's the way I want to tell the story now—as if it were happening for the first time.

My mother read the letter once more. "So?" she asked. "What are you going to do now?"

I shrugged my shoulders. "I don't know," I said. "I have to think about it."

Later, at the end of the book, I'll decide what I'm going to do.

But that comes later. First comes this.

1

Suddenly there she is. On the other side of the street, leaning against the lamppost.

A fat girl with blond curly hair. It looks so weird: such a gorgeous head of hair on such a dumpy body. The two things just don't go together.

She's leaning against the lamppost and watching the kids play, just like I'm doing. And she's watching me. I peek over at her every now and then, and when I do she always looks away.

The next day she's there again, in exactly the same place.

She looks. I look. We look.

Then Rory says to Sam and Len, "Want to play monkey in the middle?"

The boys nod.

"Who wants to be the monkey?" asks Rory. Tall, skinny, pale Rory.

He looks at the fat girl leaning against the lamppost. She nods and walks over to the boys. I hold my breath. Next thing you know, the ball comes smashing into her lower legs. Without saying a word she picks it up and tosses it to Rory.

And he throws it right back at her, as hard as he can. She doesn't seem to feel it. She picks up the ball and throws it to Rory.

Bang! This time she throws the ball to Len. He hesitates, the ball in his hands, then throws it to Rory. Once again, Rory slams the ball into her lower legs. Slowly she reaches down, picks the ball up, and walks over to Rory. She hands him the ball.

"Play again tomorrow?" she asks in a friendly way.

Not a glimmer of fear.

"Fine with me," Rory sneers with a mean-sounding laugh.

As soon as she turns her back, he puts his index finger to his temple and gives it a little twist, grinning at Len and Sam.

The next day exactly the same thing happens. She comes, and Rory throws, as hard as he can.

I can hardly bear to watch, but I can't run away, either. I *have* to see this.

After handing the ball to Rory on the second day, she doesn't walk to the lamppost on her side of the street. She comes to stand next to me.

I don't say anything. What am I supposed to say?

She stands next to me for a long time, silent. Then she turns around slowly and disappears into the bakery.

A little while later she comes out with a muffin. She gobbles it down. I can hear her smack her lips.

As soon as she's finished, she goes back into the bakery.

She comes out again and starts in on a second muffin. Then she casually produces another one and gives it to me. I grab it and take a bite. It's still warm. We eat our muffins in silence.

The next day she's standing next to the lamppost in front of the bakery. Hey, wait a minute. That's my place. She's standing in my place. But she makes room for me and hands me a muffin as if it were the most natural thing in the world.

We stand there looking. We're looking at Rory, Len, and Sam. Looking and eating. That's all.

They're playing a kind of hide-and-seek. But this hide-and-seek doesn't stop when you find the person. You've got to catch him, too. They play this game every day.

There's not much else to do in town and in the neighborhood. I come here every day to watch them, and I know how fast that pale Rory can run. He's no good at finding a hiding place, though. Too impatient.

He usually picks the same spot. Every time I come to watch I hope they'll let me play, too. I'd sneak right up on Rory and find him and catch him at the same time.

The boys whisper a little among themselves. Then Rory slowly walks up to me. I'm sure he's going to say something nice.

Rory is standing in front of me. He looks at my shoes for a minute, the shoes that he and the other boys made fun of not long ago, and asks me nonchalantly, "Want to play?" He has a nice voice. Deep.

"Play?" I repeat, trying to sound just like him. "Why?"

"Forget it, then," says Rory. He turns around and walks away.

"Okay," I shout at his back. I start running after him.

He doesn't look at me but calls to the rest of the group, "Dizzy is it."

They scatter in all directions and catch me off guard. I've always been slow. Even my report card says *Slow*.

I walk around, looking for them. Rory isn't in his normal place. The rest of the group have disappeared, too. After fifteen minutes I haven't been able to find any of them.

I've been to all the regular hiding places: behind the wall, along the railroad tracks, past the chemical-factory fence, where there's a sign with a skull on it and DANGER written underneath in big letters.

"They took off," says a voice behind me.

I turn around.

It's her. Her curls are bouncing around her head.

"Oh," I say. I say that a lot, especially when I don't know what I'm supposed to say.

"On purpose," she says. "They probably planned it ahead of time. They ditched you." She says it slowly, as if she enjoys it.

"Oh," I say again.

My head is getting light and I can see stars in front of my eyes. The world starts spinning a little.

This happens to me all the time, which is why everyone calls me *Dizzy*. I blink.

"I don't like them, either," she says.

I look at her. She's leaning against the sign that says *danger*.

I walk up to her. She has pretty teeth. Very white.

"I'm in school with them," she says. "In their class."

I nod. That makes sense. If she's not in my class then she must be in theirs. There are only two schools in our town.

"Are they always like that?" she asks.

"Like what?"

"So rotten?" She keeps trying to look at me. She can't, though, because I'm looking over her. I can see everything over her head. But I do nod. So she sees me nodding.

"Want to go to my house?" she asks, grabbing me by the arm. "I'm fucking thirsty."

She pinches me.

I nod.

"Piggy," she says as we walk along. She keeps looking straight ahead.

"Where?" I ask. There are never any pigs around here. I can't see a single one.

"Piggy," she says again, with her plump hand on her chest.

Now I get it.

"Dizzy," I tell her. "Rhymes with *Lizzy*. That's my name."

2

"Lizzy? Lizzy!" says my mother sharply.

I snap out of my daydream. I've come back to earth.

"We've really got to go now or we'll be late," says my mother.

I brush my hair one more time. Quickly. We have to be on time. It's bad enough as it is.

"Your hair looks fine," says my mother. "Just come on." She takes the car keys and holds the door open for me.

I sigh. I get in.

I try not to think about anything. I just look outside and try to remember what I'm seeing. Otherwise I'll start to dream. It happens automatically.

But now I'm going to look outside and remember. It's the only way I can get through this. Period.

We drive through the center of town. I see the supermarket cars parked behind the store, as usual.

On the square next to the church are a few old men standing in a semicircle, looking at the ground. They're tossing horseshoes.

The streets we drive through are almost empty. Everybody

is at work around this time, or they're indoors. The roll-down shutters at the local bar—it's called Up in the Clouds—are still closed.

We're supposed to go past my square and past Piggy's white house, but my mother goes another way.

I don't care. Piggy isn't there anyway. She's on her way, just like me.

"Oh no!" says my mother with irritation. A garbage truck stops right in front of us and the garbage man jumps out.

She honks.

He waves enthusiastically.

Please don't talk, I say to myself.

She waves back and lowers the window.

"Mike," she calls. "Mike, can we go past? We're sort of in a hurry."

"Sure," says Mike.

He goes to the front of the truck and shouts something to the driver, who pulls the truck over to the side.

My mother proceeds with caution. We drive past Mike. He has a stubbly chin.

The smell of decay drifts in from the garbage truck. It stings my nose. *Ignore it*, I say to myself. *Act as if you were standing on the moon and looking down.*

"Thank you," says my mother to Mike.

"You're welcome," says Mike cheerfully.

My mother shuts the window and steps on the gas. "I'm going to go talk to him first, honey," she says.

"I know that, Mom," I tell her. She's already said every-thing so many times.

That everything I say should be the truth. That later on during the interrogation I'll be all by myself. That what I did is not wrong at all. That they'll understand why I did it.

"What *we* did," I always say then. "*We* did it. I would never have done it myself."

"I know that, but in the talking room it's all going to be about what *you* did. And not about what Piggy did."

"Interrogation," I say. "What goes on in the *interrogation* room is called *interrogation*. That's what Lieutenant Dirks said on the phone, that detective guy."

"That's right," says my mother, and she bites her lower lip. My mother always bites her lower lip when she wants to say something but she doesn't know what. Or how.

So first my mother's going to talk to the detective who's going to interrogate me.

I'm used to this, my mother wanting to take new people aside and whisper something in their ear. Afterward the people look as if she hadn't said anything. As if they didn't even hear what my mother said. But usually they're a little nicer afterward. So I just let her talk.

"Will Piggy's father be bringing her?" my mother asks as we walk through the entrance.

"I don't know," I say. My face feels tight. My skin is tin-gling. I can really feel my heart. It's beating a mile a minute. *Ka-boom. Ka-boom.*

We walk to the desk. My mother says, "Lizzy Bekell and her mother for Lieutenant Dirks."

The police officer in the blue uniform makes a phone call. She laughs. "My phone is acting so strange. It makes this weird sound whenever you move it. Hear that?" She shakes the receiver back and forth wildly. What does she hear, an echo? Why is she laughing? I don't get it. I don't get *her*, which isn't unusual.

The police officer puts the receiver down and says to us, "Just a minute, he's on his way." She leans over toward us.

I can smell her bad breath—garlic and cigarettes—and I try as hard as I can not to pay any attention.

That's the way it is, I say to myself. *Period.*

"Is Piggy here already?" I ask.

"Piggy?" repeats the police officer.

"She's asking about her girlfriend," my mother explains. "She's asking about Peggy, a girl. She calls her *Piggy*. She's supposed to be here, too. Same age."

The police officer behind the desk checks her list. "She hasn't reported in yet," she says.

Lieutenant Dirks comes down the stairs. He has short gray hair and glasses. Halfway down he stops and calls, "Lizzy?" He has a nice voice. I can hear it. Deep.

I look up. Everything's spinning. I see stars everywhere. My mother takes me by the elbow.

"Come on, honey," she says.

3

She lives in the big white house. I thought it was still empty.

It's been empty for years. Sometimes the older kids break in during the summer and have parties and do other things, things we only whisper about.

The kitchen is still pretty bare.

"Did you just move in here?"

"Yes," says Piggy. She's already drunk a quart of Coke. She burps loudly and takes another bottle. She gives me a quick look. "You want some, too?"

I look at the floor tiles. "No."

"Great, 'cause I'm fucking thirsty. Really thirsty, I mean," says Piggy. "My father wants me to be a decent girl and to use decent language."

"Oh," I say.

"And I can be decent and sweet and nice sometimes, but not for long. Not long enough, at any rate."

"Oh," I say again.

"Want to see the rest of the house?" Piggy asks. I nod.

She walks out of the kitchen and into the white hallway with its high ceiling and leads me up the stairs. For such a chubby kid she's very nimble and energetic. When we get upstairs she points to the right. "The bathroom." I take a few steps down the hall and look inside. White tiles, white bathtub, white sink. White toilet. A few towels carelessly tossed on the floor. It smells like pee—and expensive soap.

Piggy walks in and picks up the towels, sighing. "And he wants *me* to be neat," she says. She hangs the towels on a rack. "You got any hobbies, Dizzy?"

I think for a minute. I don't have any hobbies. Unless you call looking a hobby. And dreaming. Looking and dreaming. "Playing outside," I mumble.

"With who?" she asks.

I don't say anything. Nobody from my school lives here in town. They come in the morning by bus and go back home in the afternoon by bus. Nobody from town plays with me.

Piggy opens a door. "My room," she says. It's a big bedroom with only a bed in it. All the clothes are lying in neat stacks in the closet. The bed looks as if no one has slept in it.

Piggy opens another door. She waves her hand. "My dad's," she says. There's a big bed in the room. The bed is covered with clothes. The bedspread is crooked and half of it is lying on the floor. Piggy closes the door before I can see anything else.

"The rest isn't interesting," she says and leads me downstairs, back to the kitchen.

Piggy raises the second bottle to her mouth and chugs down the Coke. She burps again. "I've got the lead in the school play," says Piggy nonchalantly. "Just one week at school and I've already got the lead. Imagine. I love acting. Acting onstage. At my last school I wasn't allowed to be in the play. It was really ridiculous. But I am here. I think this teacher knows talent when he sees it."

"That's great," I say.

"That's why they hate me, those jerks out there." She gestures with her chin toward the square. "But I don't like them, either."

"Oh," I say.

She changes the subject so fast. At school they talk about things much longer. First they talk about it, then they explain it, then they explain it some more, and finally they write about it.

My mother is always very calm when she does anything. But Piggy is fast.

"I'm not waiting for them. I'll decide for myself who I want to be friends with," she says. "Actually I've got friends everywhere because we move all the time."

She walks into the living room. I see a big painting, a smooth wooden floor, and white curtains. An enormous sofa and a piano. Nothing else.

Piggy sits down at the piano. She starts to play. She seems to just pull things out of the air, the beginning of one song and then the beginning of another, until she plays them both together and they become one piece. Her plump arms and hands become light, almost like butterflies. And the music ...

Supersensitive. That's what they say about me. But you

don't have to be supersensitive to know that this is good, fantastic even. As soon as I hear it I get goose bumps all over. And I'm sure other people would have the same reaction.

Piggy stops and turns on the piano bench toward me. "What school do you go to?"

"Evergreen Hills," I tell her.

"Never heard of it."

"It's a special school."

Piggy groans. "A retard."

"I'm not a retard," I say. "I'm special." That's the answer my mother taught me. I want to add that I'm smart—in some things, that is—but Piggy has already started talking.

"I'm special, too," says Piggy, "but *I* go to a regular school."

"Oh" is what I say. *Not nice* is what I think.

Piggy gets a faraway look in her eyes. She seems to be thinking about something. Suddenly she looks sad. And alone. "Joke," she says.

"You sure can play the piano," I say.

"Yes," says Piggy. "I also love horses."

"Oh."

She looks me straight in the eyes.

I'm scared to death of horses. They snort and they jerk their head up just when you think it's coming down, and the other way around. When I'm standing next to a horse, I'm afraid it's going to step forward and give me a kick. Or step backward and give me a kick. You never know what they're going to do. And if they get scared they want to run away.

"Do you love horses, too, Dizzy?"

I think as fast as I can. This is it. I've got to give the right answer or she'll laugh at me. But my head is empty. "I hate them."

Piggy starts laughing. "That's good: you either hate something or you love it. You know what I hate?" Her eyes get smaller, her face gets hard. "When people call me *Margaret*. That's my real name. That's what my father calls me, too." She stares fiercely at the white wall. "I really hate that."

Suddenly my mouth goes dry. "Can I have something to drink?"

We walk back to the kitchen. She pours what's left into a glass. A tiny bit of Coke. I drink it down.

"All we've got left is Adam's ale," she says.

I don't understand. I look at her and wait for her to explain. She turns on the tap and turns it off and then I get it. I drink as if I hadn't had anything to drink in hours.

"We're always fighting," says Piggy, "my father and me."

I can't stand fights, and I can see that she wants to tell me what the fights are about and ask me what I think, and I don't want to do that because that doesn't solve anything.

"In our part of town everybody gets mad at this one group of boys from the city," I blurt out.

Piggy lets out a piercing laugh. "What do you mean?"

"They get drunk and come out here and hassle everybody they meet."

Piggy laughs again.

It's nothing to laugh about. The kitchen starts spinning. When things start spinning, you're supposed to focus on one spot and wait until the spinning stops. Stay right where you are, don't move.

I take a deep breath. "They piss on everything. And they look for fights. Then they just pick on somebody and beat him up."

"What do you want to do now?" Piggy asks suddenly.

"Don't know," I say, but the question makes me happy. Possibilities. An ocean of possibilities. To Do Things Together.

"Let's think of a plan." Piggy thinks, and while she's thinking she sticks her tongue into the opening of the bottle to lick out the last drop.

After a while she smiles. "How about looking for eggs and pricking holes in them and blowing out the insides?" She rinses the bottle out and puts it in a basket with other empty bottles. "Or going to the park and setting it on fire? Or looking for an anthill and squashing it flat?"

I look at her with alarm.

"Joke," she says.

I laugh with relief.

She slaps me on the shoulder. "So you're a special girl," she says. "This is going to be fun!"

4

"Lizzy?"

This is something most people aren't good at: waiting.

But I am.

In the supermarket, for instance, I always choose the line with the most people in it. Then I can peek at the girl behind the cash register. I can see she's only just started working there. She wants to do a good job, but things keep going wrong. Like the stickers on the bags of fruit won't scan right. It's better if you take the stickers off and stick them back on after you've scanned them.

But she doesn't know that yet. She's only just started working there.

I breathe in the smell of the person standing in line in front of me. Sometimes it's nice. Sometimes it's sour or sweaty. I look at the shopping carts to see what people have bought. I smile at the little kids sitting in the shopping-cart seats.

"Lizzy? Lizzy!"

•

I also like to stand at bus stops. Waiting for a bus that I don't have to catch and walking away when it pulls up.

Sometimes I do the same thing in the hospital. I bike to the hospital in the afternoon and walk into the entrance, and I just sit down in the waiting room. I pick up a magazine, hum, look at the other people waiting there. I make up stories about what sicknesses they have, why they've come. What they're practicing to say to the doctor later on.

My mother is always telling me, "Sweetheart, you've got to join in more. Don't always stand on the sidelines and look at how other people live."

But I think that's stupid. Watching from the sidelines is living, too.

Just like my grandma, who always thinks it's so terrible if I sleep too long. "You're sleeping the day away," she says.

But when you dream, you're still living, still experiencing things. Why is that less valuable than all the things you experience with your eyes open?

"Lizzy!" Dirks is standing right in front of me.

I look up. My mother is standing next to him.

"We're ready," says my mother.

When you're waiting, there's always a point when the waiting is over. That's it.

When I'm sitting in a waiting room, the moment comes when it's almost my turn. There's no one else ahead of me and I've already been waiting awhile—that is *the* moment to get up. Whether it's at the dentist or the doctor or the hospital, it doesn't matter.

At a bus stop it's different. If only one bus stops at that stop, you've got to walk away as soon as the bus pulls up. But if there are more buses, you can stand there for hours. Then the waiting isn't over until you have to go home, either to eat or because that's when you're supposed to go home.

In the supermarket it's crystal clear. It's just better to have some groceries with you, even if it's a slip for returned bottles, because when it's your turn, it's your turn.

"You can go in, young lady," says the detective.

My mother pulls me toward her a bit. She gives me a quick kiss and says, "I'm going," and then, softer, "Don't daydream too much, honey. Try to pay attention a little."

Lieutenant Dirks opens a door. The *talking room* is what my mother says.

The *interrogation room* is what I say. Period.

There's a woman detective sitting at a table, behind a computer. She smiles at me.

"Have a seat," says Lieutenant Dirks, and he points to a chair. "I'll be right with you."

The woman detective shakes hands with me. "Dykstra," she says. She sneezes.

"Dizzy," I say. "Or Lizzy, either one."

The clock has to be behind me. I hear it ticking in the little room.

I look around me. What's the fastest way out?

I've got to know.

It's easy and difficult in this room because there's only one door and no windows. So you get out by way of the door, that's easy. What's difficult is that I can't see anything else.

Where the real exit is.

Just now I was doing something, but I don't remember what it was. I was daydreaming. *Now pay attention*, I say to myself.

The walls are off-white. There's a calendar on the wall turned to the wrong month. And a child's drawing, hanging crooked. The desk fills almost the entire room. A big gray office desk with drawers. A brown office chair in front of it. The back of the chair is broken at the top and a messy bunch of brown filling is sticking out. There's a computer on the desk, a telephone, and a pencil box with pens in it. A file is lying on the desk at an angle.

I love clutter and mess. It makes me feel good. Better. Everyone is always surprised about that. They think it doesn't suit me. "You're supposed to like order, promptness, regularity," they say. But I don't. It's not black or white but gray. At least the stuff in my room looks like a lot of junk, but I know where everything is. I like that.

Dykstra sneezes again. "Sorry," she says. "I've got a terrible cold."

I nod. I want to go away. Away. Away. To my favorite spot.

•

Lieutenant Dirks comes in and sits down.

The clock behind me seems to be ticking louder. I could easily turn around and see what time it is. But I don't want to. I don't want to look at the clock. Time has to stop moving forward. It has to go back. Back to before everything happened.

5

Gym class report.

Name. *First and last name.*

Subject.

What did we do during the lesson? *What was the lesson about?*

What did you do? *Did you join in? Did you say anything?*

What did you think of the lesson? *Your opinion.*

What did you learn?

I've got to do the report. Tomorrow I have gym again. But by then I won't remember what we did the last time. Gym always goes so fast. By the time it's over and we're getting dressed in the locker room, I've already forgotten what I had just been doing in the gym.

Myrna is fat. Every week during gym I suddenly realize she's fat. The rest of the week I don't think about it. Naziha's mouth hangs open during gym. After just a few minutes, you can see this little white strand of spit drooling out of her mouth. If you get too close you can smell it sometimes. I never get too close. I heard this from Cathy.

Cathy is nice. Slow and nice. She's best friends with

Alicia. Wherever Alicia is, there's Cathy. And the other way around. Alicia always talks loud. She does everything loud. Pulls the door open, slams the door shut, swings her coat around her, throws her bag on the floor.

If Alicia wasn't there, then I'd be friends with Cathy. I'd sit next to her in class. Now I sit next to Myrna. We don't talk. I forget I'm sitting next to her at all.

Name. *First and last name.* I don't feel like doing this. Not at all. Every time I pick up the paper I start to feel dizzy. The room starts swaying back and forth and I focus on a point in the center.

Name. Lizzy Bekell.

Subject. Gym.

The teacher says she's come up with this assignment especially for me because I have problems with it. She's new here. I bet she doesn't know the rules. I thought they were supposed to help me at school

What did we do during the lesson?

We played tag. Tag with wooden sticks. You tag the person with the stick. Alicia was it.

What did you do?

I ran away.

What did you think of the lesson?

I don't want to be it. I don't want to get tagged.

What did you learn?

I didn't get tagged.

●

Piggy and I are walking to my favorite spot. It is a small, round piece of grass next to a ditch at the end of a path. The path doesn't go anywhere. Maybe it used to, but it hasn't gone anywhere for a long time. People with dogs come here sometimes, but they don't walk all the way to the end, to the field. My field.

The people in town just let their dogs off the leash along the grassy edge of the path. The dogs are allowed to run free and there are benches there. Every six months the town has a big clean-up operation. The wind, rain, and animals do the rest.

Piggy drops right on the grass.

"It's soaking wet here," I say.

"So what?" says Piggy. "I'll just put something dry on later."

I drop down, too. Next to her. The wet grass makes my back and legs cold. My clothes are damp.

We look up at the clouds. The sky.

"Do you like that, too?" I ask.

"What?" asks Piggy.

"Looking at the sky."

"Mmm," she says. She starts humming a song that has something in it about looking at the clouds.

I hum along.

At the end the singer screams and groans the last lines. I don't know why. Piggy imitates her perfectly.

We laugh.

"I sang this song onstage once," says Piggy, "at my last school."

"Really? Weren't you afraid?" I say.

"I'm not afraid of doing anything," says Piggy.

"Anything?" I ask.

"Anything," says Piggy. She stands up. She reaches out a hand and starts pulling me up. "I don't believe you're not afraid of doing anything."

She lets go of my hand and I fall back on the grass. "Ouch!" I say. I rub my aching butt and back.

"It's your own fault," says Piggy and walks away.

"How about going to your house?" says Piggy when I start walking next to her again. "I want to see your room."

"Some other time," I say. My house looks much different than hers. I rub the sore spots again with my hand.

"What do you want to do, then?"

"Go to the lamppost?"

"And do what?"

"Look."

She sighs. "Look. Don't you ever get sick of doing that? You know what? We'll just go to your house for a minute and have something to drink, and then we'll see if we still feel like going to the lamppost," says Piggy.

Just before I open the front door, Piggy stops me. "What does your mother like more, goody-goodies or bigmouths?"

"What do you mean?" I ask.

"Does your mother like it if your friends have big mouths or doesn't she?" she repeats impatiently.

"Oh," I say. I think for a minute.

What is she getting at? Does she want to know how to act? Can she make a choice?

"Just be yourself, act normal," I say. "My mother likes that."

"Natural, you mean," says Piggy.

I nod, but ... I know that a lot of times I just don't understand.

"Mom, I've brought Piggy home!"

My mother is very nice to Piggy. We drink Coke, eat cookies.

My mother makes a joke. We laugh. I know she thinks it's nice that I have a girlfriend.

"Want to go to your room now?" asks Piggy.

I stand up.

"Unbelievable," she says when she gets to the doorway. "What a pigsty!"

She looks at my table. On top there's my report for gym, underneath there are books and notebooks. Next to that there are pens, wads of paper, two pairs of scissors, empty glasses, thumbtacks, half a cookie. On the floor there are clothes, plastic bags, paper, mountains of stuff. Maybe in her eyes it's a pigsty. In my eyes it isn't. I don't want the cookie anymore, but it's a shame to throw it away. Even stale cookies are still good. Those two pairs of scissors are there because one of them doesn't cut very well. Thumbtacks always come in handy. That's easiest.

"What a huge mess!" shouts Piggy. "Go get a garbage bag. You go spend the whole afternoon at the lamppost, and I'll stay here and clean up. My fingers are itching."

There's nothing wrong with my room. Everything is fine the way it is. I don't see why Piggy is so eager to clean it up. Is she acting?

She turns around. "Where's that garbage bag?"

I mutter something and I think she's making a joke. Clean up? Who goes to somebody else's house just to clean up?

"Dizzy!" She turns around and gives me a fierce look. I turn around and walk downstairs.

On the way back I practice saying the right words. *No, don't clean up. You don't have to help me. I'll do it myself. With my mother. It's always like this. I like it this way.*

"What's that?" asks Piggy, pointing to a mountain in the left-hand corner of my room.

"Stuff," I say uncertainly.

"What's it for?"

I think for a minute. There are stuffed animals that I've snuggled with a lot, and now that I see them again I realize they're still nice. There's also a bag with Barbies and another bag with Barbies—a Barbie closet full of clothes, ski stuff, bikinis, sunglasses, and binoculars. I don't play with them anymore, but they're nice things. Expensive, too, at least that's what my mother always says.

Piggy already has the Barbie stuff in her hands. The garbage bag is open on the floor, waiting for her.

"Away?"

I sigh. I already said no, didn't I?

She dumps everything in the garbage bag.

I bend over and pull the garbage bag toward me. I take a few things out. In a flash she fills up another garbage bag and tears the next bag from the roll. I pull another full garbage bag toward me and wrap my arms around it.

"What's the matter now?" asks Piggy.

"I don't like this," I say with a sigh. I put one garbage bag against the wall and put a few things on top. Maybe she'll understand if I say it very clearly.

"It looks good here," I say. "For now."

She tries to look me in the eyes. I look far over her head. I *have* to focus on *one* spot. Otherwise I'll fall over.

"You're acting retarded," says Piggy angrily.

"I *am* retarded," I say. "You said so yourself."

"You can't find anything this way."

"Yes, I can," I say. "This is the only way I can find things."

"Dizzy, you're hopeless," she says then.

I shrug my shoulders.

"Really hopeless."

Piggy opens the only closet in my room and everything falls out—on her head, at her feet—even before I can shout no.

Piggy says an ugly word.

"I can't throw anything away," I say, looking out the window. I don't want to see her face. She's angry again. I don't want to see that she doesn't understand that I like having all this stuff around me exactly as it is.

"I can," says Piggy. "I'm real good at throwing things away, because of all that moving. Just go through all the Barbie stuff. Take everything that's broken and throw it away, right now, and if there's anything else that you know for sure you can do without, get rid of it right away. Then put the rest neatly in a box."

I sweep a few things back and forth across the floor with my foot. *Now I've got to get angry*, I say to myself. I've got to scream that I really won't do this. Otherwise she won't listen to me. She'll just keep on going.

"Stop, stop—what's that?" Piggy carefully picks it up from the floor.

"My grandpa's dagger."

"Dagger?"

I take it out of her hands and pull the flat dagger with its wavy edge out of its scabbard. When all the clothes fell out of the closet, the dagger fell out, too. It's always on the highest shelf under the clothes. I hold the dagger in front of her nose.

Piggy whistles through her teeth. "That's beautiful! Can I hold it for a second?"

I give her the dagger. She carefully runs her finger along the flat sides.

"It's very sharp," I say. But then I see she's already cut herself. There's a tiny bit of blood on the edge of the knife. She runs her finger along the sharp edge once again and it bleeds even harder.

"You're bleeding," I say.

"I see that," says Piggy calmly. She just keeps it up, running her finger along the sharp edge without blinking an eye. "It's so sharp you can't even feel it." She looks dreamily at her bleeding finger.

A shiver runs down my spine. "Don't do that!" I say. "Stop!"

She keeps going. "Stop!" I scream suddenly, as loud as I can. My voice cracks.

"Okay," says Piggy. She gives the knife back to me.

Without pausing I put the dagger back in the closet. Far away, on the shelf in the back.

"What have you got back there?" asks Piggy, peering in at the stuff still lying there.

"Little things," I say vaguely. My throat hurts from all the screaming.

"Little things," Piggy repeats. "Don't say that anymore, okay? You know who always says that? The drama teacher— you know? He has it in for me."

"Oh."

She stops cleaning. She seems to have forgotten all about it. "I think I'm too good of an actress. He can't stand that. He always has 'a few little things' to tell me. But it's a whole lot, and he's always such a jerk, the way he says it."

She stares straight ahead, as if she were far away. "He doesn't know anything about it. He's jealous," says Piggy. Suddenly she looks at me, with fierce, angry eyes. "Or maybe you're on *his* side?" she asks loudly.

"No," I say, shocked. "Why would I be? I don't even know him. Why do you think that?"

"I don't know," says Piggy. "You look so weird. As if you think I'm lying."

"Of course you're not lying," I say quickly. "I'd never believe that. You're my best friend. I'm always on your side. I'll always stand up for you." I nod slowly, as if I really mean it.

"Promise?" asks Piggy.

"Promise," I say.

"Good," says Piggy. "But I'll keep you to your word."

"Oh," I say.

6

Dykstra looks at her screen. She sneezes. That's the only movement she makes.

Lieutenant Dirks rummages through some papers.

What are they doing? Why don't they say anything?

Why can't I understand people sometimes?

I understand my mother all right, but she does her best to make it easy for me.

At Evergreen Hills, my school, I don't have any problem, either. There they usually do the same thing, every day. "Structure and Security" is printed on all the letters I bring home. But with other people, it's still hard.

I don't understand Piggy, either. She's always different, she always acts differently. Other kids on the street and at Evergreen Hills think it's annoying if I don't understand them. Piggy doesn't care.

It's still quiet in the room. Are they waiting for me to start?

"We want you to tell us how everything happened," says Dirks. "We have the report from the parents of Len and Sam. We have the declarations from Rory and Len and Sam themselves. But we also want to hear your side of the story."

I squirm in my chair. "Is Piggy here yet?" I ask.

"That other girl? Not yet," says Dirks. "They're still waiting for her."

"And what if she doesn't come?" I ask.

"Then we'll go get her," says Dykstra. "It's a serious offense."

"We've got to hear what she has to say," says Dirks.

"I want my mother to come back," I say. "I want her to be with me."

Dykstra shakes her head. "She might influence you, or us. But you already know that. She's already explained that to you very carefully. Only in very, very exceptional cases—"

"Your mother is a nice woman, Lizzy," interrupts Lieutenant Dirks. "A very nice woman."

"Yes," I say.

My mother can do things that other people can't do. At least they can't do them as well as she can. She's real good at talking softly and she has a really sweet laugh. She always says the right thing at the right time. In the back of her throat there's this cooing sound that can make you really happy. Her lips are soft, but they're strong, too. Her neck smells really, really good. Nobody's allowed to smell her there except me—and my father, of course, but not anymore.

"She hasn't had an easy time of it. Lost her husband, worried about you ... But it's been going well recently. You had a girlfriend. ..." He picks up a paper and reads: "Uh, Margaret. At your school, Evergreen Hills, a special school, everything was going fine. ..."

I hear my heart pounding in my ears. The room starts spinning.

"But now it's all taken a downhill turn because of what you did."

I stand up and stagger to the door. Away! I can't stay here. I open the door and find myself in a big room. Three people look up from their work. Behind me I hear a chair drop.

"Stop!" says Dirks. "Come back."

He grabs me from behind by the shoulders. I turn around.

"Don't touch me!" I say loudly.

"Of course," says Dirks right away and lets me go. "But then you've got to come back and sit with us. No use running away. You know that."

No escape, I say to myself. *Period*.

7

"Can you give me a hand?" asks the gym teacher as I'm walking out of school.

She's new. Sometimes she asks if I want to help. If I'll do some cleaning up after school. If I'll get things ready.

I nod.

Ever since we became friends, Piggy picks me up at school. She gets out first and walks straight over to my school. She waits till I'm out. I'm not used to that.

I'm not used to someone standing there, someone waiting for me, someone who wants to play with me. It's nice, and at the same time it takes some getting used to. Before, when I left school, I'd walk to my place next to the lamppost near the bakery to watch and listen and dream. But now there are plans. We talk about things, drink Coke at her house, straighten up her room, and get muffins from the bakery.

I quickly hand the stuff to the gym teacher. She notices, I think.

"Do you really have time?" she asks.

"Yes," I say.

She looks at me. I don't want to see how she looks at me.

"No," I say. "Not really."

"Then just say so!" she says.

I want to shut my eyes, but I don't.

At Evergreen Hills they teach me two life lessons: to face up to things and to stand outside myself.

This is how I'm supposed to face up to things: I'm not ever allowed to close my eyes when something happens that I don't like, and I'm definitely not allowed to think that this is how to make it go away. Whatever it is I'm supposed to face up to, I have to say it out loud, like, "I'm afraid to say that I don't have time." And then I have to finish by saying "period." So, "I'm afraid to say that I don't have time, period." Like that.

So I'm not supposed to stand outside myself by closing my eyes and acting like I'm not there or that "it" isn't there. I'm supposed to stand outside myself by looking at myself from a distance. Or at the things I don't like. For instance, I have to look at the garlic smell from someone's mouth— which I think is disgusting—as if I were living on the moon and looking down at the earth. Or I have to act as if I were watching myself and the other person on TV. And then they want me to laugh at it.

I still can't do this very well. Not at all, actually.

I don't live on the moon. I'm not on TV. I can't laugh at something that's not nice.

"What's the worst thing you've ever done, Dizzy?" Piggy asks me as we walk away from my playground.

"The worst?" I repeat. *I have no idea*, I say to myself.

"Think a minute. Come on, slowpoke, you must have done something that you weren't supposed to do." Piggy gives my shoulder a shove.

I take a step away from her. "No touching," I say.

The worst, I say to myself.

The worst is that once I kept on riding my bike with a flat tire. I came bumping down the road, and when I got home I was afraid at first to say what I had done. My mother saw there was something wrong and asked me what it was. I told her. My front wheel was all crooked because of it.

I started to cry. My mother comforted me. She bought a secondhand front wheel from Mr. Hooker and now my bike's okay.

"Well, what is it? The worst?" Piggy asks impatiently.

"Biking with a flat tire," I tell her.

"Oh, how awful!" says Piggy.

I'm shocked. She says it as if it's really terrible.

"Joke," she says. "It's just good that you don't know what the worst thing was that *I* did."

"What was it?"

"You don't know, that's just what I said."

We're standing by the lamppost. I'm looking at the sky. The kids. The game. It makes me feel calm. It's familiar.

"Shall we go to the market?" asks Piggy.

"Why?" I ask.

"Because," says Piggy. "It's boring here."

"It's boring at the market, too," I say.

"You don't know that," says Piggy, "'cause we're standing here." She looks at me. Her white teeth flash. "Right?"

I nod. Shake my head. Nod. Why do you always have to say either yes or no?

"Why do you always want to look at those stupid kids?"

I don't say anything. What am I supposed to say?

"You want to play dumb? Fine, then I'm leaving." Piggy starts walking away, slowly, step by step.

She turns around.

I'm standing by the lamppost.

She takes a few more steps, turns around.

I sigh. I push myself away from the lamppost and walk toward her.

"Today you're going to get even with them all," she says as I start walking beside her.

"What?" I ask. "What am I going to get even for?"

"All that teasing. That they're always so rotten to you."

"Oh," I say. "But how?" I really don't want to know. It just slips out.

"I have a plan," says Piggy.

She leans over and whispers into my ear. It tickles. I want to turn my head away, but Piggy has her hands clamped around my upper arm.

It's a good plan.

"I don't know," I say. "I don't care."

"You're scared," says Piggy.

"Maybe," I admit.

"Chicken," says Piggy.

"Whatever," I say, trying to struggle out of her grip. She squeezes even harder. "Let me go!" I shout.

Piggy gives my arm a jerk. She accidentally touches my head.

"Don't touch my head!"

Right away Piggy grabs my head with her two hands and holds on tight. "You have to go along with my plan," she says. "If you don't go along with it, you're against me."

I try to laugh, but my laugh doesn't sound happy. I can hear it. And this is no joke.

Piggy's hands squeeze. Hard. Harder. My head is almost bursting. *I'm* almost bursting. She has to stop! But she's behind me.

Kick her, I say to myself. *Kick back, like a horse.* I try it. She easily steps out of the way. She knows what I wanted to do.

I'm strong, but not strong enough.

We go into the bike shop. Old Mr. Hooker slowly walks up to us. He always takes his time.

"Hello, Lizzy," he says in a friendly voice. "I haven't seen you in a while. How's it going?"

"Fine," I say. "And how are you?"

"Great," he says, "for such a rusty old velocipede." He grins. "Can I do something for you two?"

He looks at Piggy with curiosity.

"Well," I say. "This is my girlfriend, Piggy. She lives in the white house—you know, the one that was empty for so long."

Mr. Hooker nods at Piggy. She grins back. White teeth.

"Now we want to go for a bike ride. ..."

Here's where the lie comes, I say to myself. *Right here. Try to sound convincing.* I take a deep breath. I see stars. The shop starts spinning. "But she lost her bike key during the move and she can't open the lock." There it is. I wait.

"So we want to buy a new lock and borrow a hacksaw to saw the old one open," Piggy says now.

Mr. Hooker walks to the wall where the locks are hanging. "Plenty to choose from," he says.

Piggy points to a padlock with a strong steel chain. Mr. Hooker walks to his ancient cash register and types in the amount.

We pay, but we don't leave.

"How's your mother, Lizzy? Everything okay?"

I nod. We still don't leave.

"Anything else?" asks Mr. Hooker.

"The hacksaw," says Piggy.

"Oh, right," says Mr. Hooker. He shuffles to the back of the shop, rummages a bit through his tools, and comes back with a dusty hacksaw in his hand. "If you use it to do something you're not supposed to, don't tell me." He laughs at his own joke.

We hurry out of the shop. "What an old fart!" says Piggy when we get outside.

We walk to the old train tracks. Under the tracks there's a small tunnel that was made long ago, maybe for bicycles and pedestrians. Other people say it's a crossing for frogs and toads. At any rate, the tunnel hasn't been used for years. It's closed off with a rusty lock.

Piggy saws off the lock like a pro. We take a step inside. All sorts of live things scurry away from our feet. It smells musty, like stagnant water, encrusted spider webs, and dried-out lizards. I shiver. We step back outside and close off the tunnel with our new lock.

"How about stopping off at your house?" asks Piggy as we walk toward the bike shop. "I'm fucking thirsty."

"Let's take this back first." I swing the hacksaw back and forth.

"What's the hurry?" asks Piggy. "How many people does he get every day who need a hacksaw?"

"Yes, but I told Mr. Hooker—" I sputter in protest.

Piggy interrupts me. "I want to go to your house," she says. "You told him you'd bring it back, but you didn't say when." Piggy grabs my arm again and pinches till it hurts. "Come on, let's go see your mother and get something to drink. I'm thirsty."

"Okay," I say reluctantly. "Then we'll return the saw, right before closing time."

Piggy sighs. "Do you always have to get your way?"

And how about you? I say to myself. But not out loud. I don't like to quarrel.

8

"I'm going to ask you a few questions, Lizzy," says Dirks. "You're not required to answer them. You have the right to remain silent. It makes everything easier if you cooperate. But you don't have to do that."

"Oh," I say.

"Do you understand?"

"Yes," I say.

"Whose idea was it?" asks Dykstra. She tries to look in my eyes. I look just over her head.

I can hear the clock. I can hear the humming of the computer. But the sound of the clock is louder. I count with it. Twenty-one, twenty-two, twenty-three ...

At school they say that counting to yourself calms you down. If you feel really rattled, it helps, counting to yourself. Twenty-four, twenty-five. I'd like to count my way to the exit. Keep calm.

But I have to stay here. They can keep me for six hours, according to the law. That's what my mother said. Six hours. That's a long time. I want to go home. Or to my favorite spot.

I can hear the clock ticking. I've lost count.

"I didn't do it," I say.

Lieutenant Dirks frowns.

"*We* did it. We. Piggy and me. If it hadn't been for her ..."
I start crying. The sobs come up from deep in my stomach.
My breathing is irregular. I can't stop.

"It was a mistake. I made a terrible mistake," I say, my
voice trembling. "My mother always says that if you make
terrible mistakes you have to be forgiven. Things like that
happen, she says. Sometimes you can make up for them."

Dykstra pours me a glass of water. I gulp it down. I
swallow the wrong way. I start coughing.

"Take it easy," says Lieutenant Dirks. "It may look as if we
want to put all the blame on you, but that's just not true. You
can be sure of that. We only want you to tell us what exactly
happened. According to you."

I sniffle again, but more softly this time.

Dykstra says, "You don't have to be afraid of us. We're
really not mad at you. We only want to hear the truth."

Dirks clears his throat. "That's our job, find out what the
truth is."

A shiver goes down my spine.

"You know I've just spoken with your mother," Dirks goes
on. "Your mother says you're usually a nice, peaceful girl, and
I believe that. You're smart in some things. Most of the time
you were alone, until you got to know Margaret. You became
good friends in a very short time, didn't you?"

I shake my head yes.

"Do you mean you weren't friends?" Dirks asks.

I shake my head. "Blood sisters," I say. "We're blood sisters."

Dykstra looks up. "What do you mean exactly?"

I press one finger against another. "Blood," I say.

"Oh," she says.

Dirks asks, "Just tell me, what happened that night?"

I grab my head.

The world is moving. I see all these dots before my eyes. I once saw a painting that was all dots. Big and little, some close together and some farther apart. If you stand up close, that's all you can see. If you stand farther away, you can see what it's supposed to be.

A landscape with birds and water. I remember that I kept going closer and then stepping back. Up close you just couldn't believe that—

"Lizzy?" It's the stuffed-up voice of Dykstra, cutting through my daydream.

"Why did you do it?" asks Dirks.

The wall in front of me is an ocean of dots. I've got to pay attention, my mother says. Don't dream too much. But I don't want to be here. "I don't want any more questions," I say and start staring at the wall. "You understand?"

If I hold my head very still, it will all go away.

"She's shut us out," Dirks says to Dykstra after a while.

I stare at the wall.

"Just a minute," says Dirks. He winks at Dykstra and they go out.

Soon Dykstra comes back alone. "Lieutenant Dirks has other things to do," she says. "We'll continue alone, just the two of us. That's better, I think. Don't you?"

9

"Mom, we're going out for a minute," I say. I stand up.

Piggy stands up, too. "That was delicious Coke, ma'am," she says.

My mother laughs. "Have fun outside," she says. "And be home by six o'clock, okay?"

Come on! I say to myself, following Piggy. *This is how you can get even with them once and for all. They've always been really mean.*

The fact is that my legs don't want to go that way.

But the same thing keeps ringing in my ears: *here's your chance.*

I walk into Mr. Hooker's shop with the hacksaw in my hand. Piggy loiters outside the door.

"Problem solved?" asks Mr. Hooker.

I nod and give him back the hacksaw.

"You happy with your school?" he asks.

I nod. Mr. Hooker is never in a hurry.

"And now you've got a girlfriend, too. That's great," says Mr. Hooker.

I fiddle with my clothes. I'm not very good at this, having a casual conversation. Piggy's much better at it than I am. My head is empty. "How's your wife?" I ask.

Mr. Hooker gives me a strange look. "My wife isn't alive anymore," he says softly.

I draw in my breath. Of course! I knew that. Mrs. Hooker always sat inside at the window in the apartment over the shop. But suddenly she wasn't there anymore.

"I'm sorry," I say. "I'm really, really sorry." That's all I can think of.

"You like it here?" Mr. Hooker calls to Piggy in a hoarse voice.

Piggy walks in. "Yes," she says, "especially now that we're such good friends."

I can tell I'm blushing. We don't say things like that out loud around here.

"I just saw a whole group of big boys. I don't think they're from around here," says Piggy. "When we were sawing through my bike lock. They made a lot of noise."

"Are they back again, those troublemakers?" asks Mr. Hooker.

I don't know where to look. I didn't see anything. Why did she say that?

Piggy gives Mr. Hooker a radiant smile. "We've got to go," she says and walks out. I hurry behind her.

My knees feel very weak.

"There," says Piggy, outside. "Later on probably the whole town will know that those creeps are back in the neighborhood!"

"Why do they have to know that?"

She looks at my face. "Our plan, you idiot, our plan. The more scared they are, the better."

"Oh," I say.

"I think you could use something nice," says Piggy. "Wait a minute."

She walks away, turns around, and walks back. "Wait here! Even if it takes a long time, stay here. I'll come back later with something nice."

I watch her as she walks away. I lean against the wall. Even if I wanted to, I wouldn't be able to leave. I sigh. I'm so tired. So tired.

After a long time, she comes back with a flat white box in her hands.

"Ta-da!" she says, flopping on the ground. "Come, look, and eat."

I sit down next to her. She pushes the box in my hands.

It's a cake. A cake from our bakery. An enormous cake with white icing, and it's got our names written on it, connected. Above the *I* in *DIZZY* there's a big *P* and under it *GGY*.

"For you," she says. "You do pretty well for a retard."

I'm so angry, I want to give the cake back to her and jump to my feet, but she's already got a strong grip on my shoulder. It's as if she knew what I was going to do before I did it.

"Joke," she says. She points to the *I* connecting our two names. "We have a lot in common, don't we?" Then she grabs the side of the cake and starts to pull. "If only we had your knife," she says. "That dagger." She pushes a sloppy chunk into my hands.

I start eating.

She grabs an even bigger piece for herself, pushes it against mine, and says, "To us, to our friendship."

We eat until half the cake is gone.

"I feel sick," I say.

"Me, too," says Piggy. "Sick as a dog. But we've got to finish it." She takes another bite and burps.

I laugh.

"It's not funny," says Piggy. "You're either in or you're out."

I keep laughing.

"What's the matter, Dizzy? What's so funny?" Piggy gives me an angry look. Her mouth is full of white icing. "I didn't think so!" Her voice is sharp and loud. "Nothing's funny. Nothing at all, you moron."

I'm not laughing anymore.

Piggy tears off another piece of cake. She jams it into my mouth. The icing fills my nose. It sticks to my cheeks.

"Eat!" she says sharply and pushes the cake in harder.

I take a bite. Wipe off my cheeks, lick up the icing. She looks at me. Suddenly she smiles.

"Joke?" she says with a questioning look.

When the cake is finished, she stands up. "Now I'm fucking thirsty. Let's go to my house and get something to drink."

"My father wants me to act decently," says Piggy. She's leaning against the nice clean counter and rubbing her stomach. "You want something to drink, too?" She starts looking for a second bottle.

I shake my head.

"Aren't you ever thirsty?" Piggy narrows her eyes into little slits. "Maybe you're not human. Maybe you're a machine."

She taps my back, my belly, my legs, my head, examining me all over.

I tighten up. "Don't do that," I say loudly. "And don't touch my head!" I step aside. Fast.

"Take it easy, calm down," says Piggy. "No, you're not a machine. Machines don't care where you touch them." Then with a gloomy voice she says, "My father would be overjoyed if I were a machine. Overjoyed! Then he'd be able to program me just the way he wants: don't talk loud, don't burp, don't curse, don't be so fat, don't be fresh. He'd be able to input it all."

"I don't know if you can input *don't* things," I say. "I don't think so."

"What do you mean?" asks Piggy.

"I think you can only input what you want: be polite, be thin, talk nice."

"Hey, don't start getting smart on me. That's my job," says Piggy.

But I'm smart, too, I say to myself. *In some things. Can't I let it show sometimes?*

Piggy sees a fly in the kitchen. She follows it with her eyes like a predator following its prey. As soon as it lands, she moves her hand toward it very slowly. "If you move real slow, the fly won't notice how close you are," she says. "Its eyes aren't made to notice. Then you can squish it."

She squishes. There's a crunching sound.

I shiver. "Where is your father anyway?" I ask quickly. "What kind of work does he do?"

Piggy sighs.

She walks to the piano in the living room and I walk behind her. I feel relieved and happy. She's going to play!

Piggy strikes a few chords. Right away that amazing sound gives me goose bumps.

She plays a very slow song, with something running through it that doesn't belong there. She stops. "My father works for the government," says Piggy. "What he does is secret, so we have to move a lot." She keeps on playing. "He's almost never home, and that's fine with me."

Piggy plays something lively, fast and simple. "Because when he's home we always fight," says Piggy. She slaps the keys with the palms of her hands and slams the piano shut.

I jump. "I have to go home," I say.

"Oh no you don't, Dizzy," says Piggy. She stands up and walks slowly toward me.

"I really do," I say. "It's ten to six."

"But you have to help me," says Piggy. "Go over my lines."

"You were there when my mother said six o'clock. And it takes at least ten minutes to walk to my house. ..." I hear my voice starting to sound like I'm begging. It happens automatically.

"Are you my friend?" asks Piggy, standing right in front of me.

I nod.

"My best friend?" she asks again, and I nod.

"If your best friend needs you, you can't walk out on them, can you?" asks Piggy. "You can't just abandon your best friend!" She takes another step forward while she's standing right in front of me. I take a step backward, and then another.

I help her go over her lines. On the couch in the empty white living room.

She doesn't know the text very well. I have to keep prompting her.

"Again," she says. And I repeat it.

"Again," she says, and I say it again.

Slowly the text makes its way into her head. Every now and then I have to prompt her with a word or correct her. After half an hour I stand up and put the script on the couch.

"What are you doing?"

"I'm going home," I say.

"No," she says. She stands up and pushes me back.

"Cut it out," I say. The couch is hard. My voice is soft. Too soft.

I pick up the script and start in again. After three sentences I put it down.

"My mother is waiting for me. She's going to start to worry."

"So what?" says Piggy.

"I don't want to quarrel," I say. I shake my head.

"So call her," she says.

I nod, shake my head. "I want to go home," I say. My heart is pounding. *Ka-boom. Ka-boom.* "I want to go home *now*."

Piggy looks angry. I can feel it. This time I have to insist. This time I have to be clear. "And I don't want to get even with them. Why should I?"

Piggy stands up and throws my jacket at me. "Okay, we're all talked out," she says. "If that's the way you want it, fine with me. Go ahead and stand there alone all the time watching those stupid kids. Let them tease you till you're old and gray. I don't care. Hurry home to your mommy. See you later—much later." She pushes me out the door.

Astonished, I put on my jacket outside.

Then I wait for a minute on the front stoop.

She starts playing the piano. I listen.

She plays as loud as she can, banging on the keys. It goes on and on: the same notes, really loud and really fast. Then she adds something to make it extra awful, which is just what it's supposed to be.

Suddenly she stops and it's quiet for a long time. I want to walk away, but I keep standing there.

She starts playing again. Softer, slower, with prettier notes sprinkled in between. Almost a song. But every time it gets a little nicer, she starts in again with that loud, awful music.

10

I stand up and walk to the door. Calmly.

"What are you doing?" asks Dykstra.

"I'm leaving," I say. "I've said enough. I don't want to be here anymore."

"Lizzy, I want everyone to tell the whole story," says Dykstra. "If you leave now, I'll have to put *incomplete interrogation* in your file. I hate doing that. Do me a favor. Just sit down and keep talking."

I sit down.

Silence.

"Talk at your own speed, Lizzy. In your own way."

I don't know what I'm supposed to say. If she asks a question, I can answer it. How am I doing? How did you get to know each other? When did you meet? What do you do together? Is it fun?

"I don't know," I say.

"Take your time," says Dykstra. She blows her nose and looks at me. I quickly look away.

It's quiet in the room. The computer is humming, the clock is ticking.

•

If I keep looking above Dykstra's head, I can imagine starlings flying there. Just as many as I sometimes see from my bedroom window.

In our yard there's only one tree. Every year it gets little red berries on it. Every year my mother says she wants to get rid of it. It cuts out the sunlight, she says then. The berries are poisonous for children, even though they look so delicious. But children never come to our house. We never sit in the yard, my mother and me. The tree will probably still be there in a gazillion years.

All the starlings want to sit in *our* tree and nowhere else. Our tree quickly fills up with birds, and they make a terrible racket. There are lots of other birds flying in the air around the tree. I'm absolutely sure that there isn't enough room for one more starling. Even so, starlings are always perching in the tree. They may make room for each other, but I can't tell. It all happens too fast, with too much noise. But there are fewer and fewer birds flying in the sky and the tree looks darker and darker.

"Lizzy?"

I keep staring over the head of Lieutenant Dykstra with deep concentration. It's all black from the thoughts in my head. Just when I think there isn't enough room for one more thought, another one comes in. Black thoughts.

"Lizzy? Will you tell me something else about that night?"

I shake my head. "She's really good at playing the piano," I say. "Beautiful and awful."

Dykstra nods. She sits up straighter and stops looking at my face.

"How do I know for sure that you won't get mad?"

"You can count on it," she says.

"Oh," I say.

Suddenly she looks very tired, and very stuffed up.

"So I can just tell you everything? It's always okay?" I ask.

She nods. She doesn't look at me.

She pulls her chair up next to me, very slowly and very carefully, until she's about a foot away from me and we're sitting side by side, looking at the same wall. As if we were both watching TV together.

"Can I tell you every little detail?"

"I wish you would," says Dykstra.

11

Piggy isn't my friend anymore.

When I get out of school she's not standing there.

Of course, I don't *want* to see if she's there, but I look at the place where she usually waits all the same. Empty. Just to be sure I look at some other places and around back. But she's really not there. The world starts spinning. Stars everywhere. I'm Dizzy.

I walk back into the school.

The classroom is empty. The buses are gone. The almost-new gym teacher is walking down the corridor. She's carrying the rings. The gym teacher gets all these wrinkles around her eyes when she laughs. Her voice is clear and friendly. She likes to eat fruit. She always has a couple of apples with her.

I walk into the corridor. I wait.

"You have time to help me again?" she asks in a friendly voice. I nod.

We walk back and forth three times. All the rings and the other stuff are put away.

She straightens out the benches in the gym. Every now and then she looks at me. I pretend not to notice. Then she sits down and starts peeling an apple.

I come closer. She gives me a piece. We eat and don't say anything. When we've eaten the whole apple, I stand up and say, "Thanks."

"Thank *you*," she says.

I walk to my lamppost and even from this distance I can see Piggy's not there.

Looking at Rory and the others isn't as nice as it used to be. Where is she?

After a long time I see her in the distance, coming closer. Slowly. My heart starts beating faster. *Ka-boom. Ka-boom.* I feel myself standing and looking. She doesn't stand next to me but starts leaning against the opposite lamppost. I pretend not to see her. She does the same.

After ten minutes I can't stand it anymore. I walk quickly to the big road. Should I go home? My mother is at work. Far away. I think about the empty living room and the empty kitchen and keep on walking, to my favorite spot.

Once I'm there I look at the wild roses and the sky.

What did I always do before I knew her?

This was all so nice then, wasn't it?

Every day I stay longer after school. I help the gym teacher.

When we sit down together on a bench, she says, "My name is Nelly." And then I suddenly realize that I never even knew her name. I nod. I push the bench against the wall with my leg. She tosses me an apple. It falls. She tosses another one. This one falls, too.

"I can't catch," I say.

"We can practice catching," says Nelly.

I shake my head.

She picks up an apple and starts peeling it effortlessly. We eat the apple together.

"Another report is coming up," says Nelly. "You're not wild about doing reports, are you?"

I shake my head. "What's it about?" I ask.

"Dodge ball," she says.

I shiver. She sees it.

"You don't like dodge ball?" asks Nelly.

I shake my head. "I hate it," I say.

Nelly laughs. "You hate throwing the ball or getting hit?"

I shrug my shoulders.

"Well?" she asks.

"Both," I say.

"I have to set up a big track for tomorrow," says Nelly. "Want to help?"

I nod.

"Alicia and Cathy are helping, too."

"Oh." I nod.

"Does that sound like fun?"

I can just picture Cathy slowly walking on the wrong side of the track and in my head I can hear Alicia make a huge racket with everything she does.

"Does that sound like fun?"

I nod. Shake my head. Nod. "If we have to do it together it will take much longer."

●

Alicia and Cathy are already in the gym by the time I get there.

"We're helping," says Cathy proudly. "The bus isn't coming to pick us up until later."

Alicia runs up, takes a jump, and screams. It echoes through the gym.

Nelly comes in. She shows us where everything has to go. Horse here, mats there, cone there, rings hanging down, get those cabinets ready, pull out the wall bars. We all pitch in and get down to work. Alicia slaps the mats down and drags the benches screeching across the floor. Nelly keeps going over to her and kindly explaining what she has to do. Cathy soon gets tired and wants to sit down. Nelly makes a deal with her: she can sit down later on and she'll get the biggest piece of apple.

When everything is ready, Nelly peels the apple. She looks at her watch. "Your bus is here," she says to Cathy and Alicia. They jump up, grab their pieces of apple, and leave.

I stand up, too.

"Wait a minute," says Nelly.

I sit back down.

"Did you enjoy having them with us?"

"I don't know," I say.

"Just tell me," says Nelly.

"I don't know," I say again. "Do you enjoy working here?"

"Yes," says Nelly, "I really enjoy teaching here."

She looks at me. I look away. "Shall we practice catching? The two of us?"

I shake my head.

She stands up anyway and gets a large, soft ball. She throws it to me and I try to catch it, but I miss. It rolls along the floor.

"You have to look at the ball, not at your hands," she says kindly.

She picks up the ball and throws it to me again. I follow the ball and it touches my hands, but I grab it too late and it falls.

"Doesn't matter," says Nelly.

I nod.

"If we keep practicing, someday you'll get it, all of a sudden. As long as you practice often. Really try. Again and again."

I nod.

"Try," says Nelly. "Everything begins with trying. With practice. Succeeding isn't the important thing—it's doing. See you tomorrow again?"

I nod.

"Only come if you really feel like it."

And that's what I find so difficult.

Outside I walk straight to my lamppost.

There she is!

Piggy is leaning against my lamppost and eating a muffin. Right away everything starts spinning so fast that I have to stop walking. Should I go and stand next to her? And what then?

"You dizzy?" she asks.

I nod. She grabs me firmly by the upper arm and pulls me more or less to the lamppost, and it feels good.

We look. She looks. I look.

Everything is quiet and fine.

She pulls a muffin out of the bag and gives it to me.

After a long time, she clears her throat. I wait to hear what she's going to say.

"Never do that again, okay?" she says hoarsely. "Just walking away like that."

But the next day after school I don't hurry outside. I know that Piggy is there, ready for step two of our plan. *Her* plan.

First I go to Nelly and grab one of the soft balls.

"Shall we practice?" she asks.

I nod.

Nelly throws and the ball keeps falling. After a while I put the ball back where I found it.

I walk to the window.

Piggy is leaning against a wall near the bike rack, and every time I look out the window to see if she's still there, she's there. She's not going away. Of course not.

"My friend is waiting," I say.

She is your friend, I say to myself. *And you want her to be your friend, don't you? Come on, go see her. Finally you've got a friend and you're still not happy. Still not satisfied,* I say to myself.

Just as I'm about to leave the gym, Nelly calls to me. I turn around.

"Very good," says Nelly. "You're practicing, that's what it's all about."

I nod. Proudly.

"Hi," I say once I'm outside. "I had something to do."

"Don't you want to know how it went with the theater thing?" asks Piggy right away.

I nod.

"So ask me, Dizzy," says Piggy.

"How did it go?" I ask.

"Shitty," says Piggy. "I knew all the lines, but that asshole drama teacher found a thousand and one 'little things' to complain about. I have to practice again tonight. And you have to help me."

It isn't a question.

"I really can't come home too late tonight," I tell her. "The last time my mother was already a little angry."

"My father is always angry," says Piggy. She pauses a minute. "Get used to it."

We walk to the supermarket and spend twenty dollars on candy. A whole mountain of colors smiles at us from the shopping cart.

"We'll use this to lure them," says Piggy with satisfaction.

At Piggy's house we get a big storage container and put all the candy inside.

We go to our lamppost. They're all playing hide-and-seek again. Piggy and I put the container between us. We look and snack, snack and look, smack our lips and snack, and quickly get the attention we were hoping for.

Rory walks up to us, his eyes narrowed into slits.

"Hey, horsey, what've you got there?" he asks.

Piggy doesn't respond.

"Candy," I say and tip the container a little so he can see what's in it.

He kneels down next to the container and takes a piece of candy. "Mmm," he says. "Is it full?"

"Yes," I tell him. "Feel."

He sticks his hand deep into the container and pulls up a few more candies, which he puts in his mouth.

"Nice, Margaret," he says. "That's not all for Dizzy and the Trojan horse, is it?"

"Of course not," says Piggy now. "Tonight we're going to play a game. It's called Chicken Feed. Be here at ten o'clock, and everything you win is for you. Everybody can play. There's plenty."

"Ten o'clock tonight? So late?" he asks.

Ten o'clock, I say to myself. My mother will never agree to that.

"Don't they let you stay out that late?" teased Piggy. "We can make it seven o'clock if you want, so you're home before bedtime."

"Ten o'clock, we'll be there," says Rory, and he turns around. "We're going to empty that container tonight and we may want to play your game again tomorrow, too."

"I don't think so," says Piggy, chuckling quietly to herself.

•

"We'll go to your house to go over my lines." She taps on the backpack holding the folder with the script. "So you won't be too late, either."

Once we get to my room she starts right in with cleaning up. After half an hour she sits down on the bare floor and slaps the space next to her with the palm of her hand.

I sit down beside her.

She takes out the script. I read the front page for the first time.

"'*The Trojan Horse*. A Trojan horse is a desirable thing that is welcomed into a place but contains hidden undesirable cargo.'"

"What does that mean?" I ask.

Piggy starts rattling off her lines. She stops. "In the beginning *The Trojan Horse* is fun, but later on it's not. Not at all, in fact," says Piggy.

"That's why Rory called you horsey," I say.

Piggy ignores my remark. "That drama teacher really gets on my nerves. What do you think I should do about it?"

"No idea," I say.

"That's no help," says Piggy angrily.

"Tell him what you think?" I squeak.

"As if that jerk would understand."

I take a deep breath. "When I was smaller, I always squeezed my eyes shut if I didn't want to see something, and that made me think it wasn't there. Sometimes I fell down or stubbed my toe because I did it when I was walking or biking. At Evergreen Hills they're teaching me to pay attention to things. At least they're trying." I bite my tongue. "So if you don't want to see something," I say, and my heart is pounding, "you can just shut your eyes."

"Thanks. I'll have to remember that," says Piggy.

She doesn't laugh at me. She doesn't make a joke. In fact, her face is quite serious.

"You know, Dizzy," says Piggy, "I think we have to do something to strengthen our friendship."

She nods at me.

"Strengthen?" I repeat. I learned that at Evergreen Hills. You can gain time by repeating the question or parts of the question.

"Indissoluble."

"Oh."

"With a ritual."

"With a ritual? What's that?"

Piggy has had enough of my questions. She stands up, walks to my closet, searches on the shelf in the back, and holds up the dagger. "A blood ritual," she says. She pulls the dagger out of its scabbard and cuts the end of her index finger. A thick drop of blood slowly appears.

"Now you." She solemnly hands me the dagger.

I hesitate. Not because I'm afraid of the pain but because I'm a little afraid of her.

"Afraid?" she asks.

I nod. Shake my head.

"You know what I'm afraid of?" she asks.

I shake my head.

"I'll tell you what I'm afraid of, then you tell me what you're afraid of. Okay?" Her voice sounds a little hoarse.

I nod.

"We have to keep moving because of my father's work," says Piggy.

I nod.

"And because we keep moving I always have to make new friends." She takes a deep breath and almost says something but brushes it aside with her hand.

"I don't get it," I say.

"That I'm all alone. And that I'll always be alone. That's what I'm afraid of," she says. "Kind of stupid to be afraid of being alone, of course, because I make friends so easily. What are you afraid of?" she asks me.

"You already know," I tell her. "Being touched. Especially my head. It makes me think that everyone knows what's going on inside my head. That they can read my mind."

Piggy takes my arm, pulls it forward, and grabs my index finger. She pushes the knife into a bit of my skin, quickly and effortlessly, and mixes my blood with hers.

"There. Didn't hurt much, did it?" she asks. "This is forever. Indissoluble. Blood sisters. We're blood sisters. We're family."

12

It's ten o'clock at night and still pretty light out. I've told my mother that I'm going to sleep at Piggy's. There are five kids standing around us—around us and the container full of candy.

"Where's the rest?" asks Piggy.

"Let's just start," says Rory.

"Yes," I agree. "Later on it'll get dark. And it looks like those city creeps are back in the neighborhood." Piggy and I have agreed that I would say this.

"City creeps?" Piggy looks very surprised. "Who are they?"

"Only somebody who's not from around here would ask a question like that," says Rory.

"Big guys who get drunk and start fights," says Len. "I'm really not supposed to go out."

"Come on, play," says Rory.

"Does everybody know the game?" asks Piggy. "We put candy in the lid, one of you goes away, and the rest of us pick one piece of candy. The one who's 'it' comes back and starts pointing to pieces of candy. He can have all the candy he picks until he points to the piece that we've already chosen, and then we shout, 'Chicken feed!' Who's going first?" She looks Rory deep in the eyes.

"Okay," he says. Piggy grabs him by the upper arm. He tries to pull himself free, but she has a firm grip on him so he walks away with her, into the darkness.

"Which one are we going to choose?" I ask. My heart is pounding in my throat. I try to let my voice sound as normal as possible.

We pick a licorice shoelace.

"Come on back!" I yell. Rory and Piggy come walking out of the darkness.

Rory starts choosing. He wins lots of candy. Finally he points to the black shoelace and everybody shouts, "Chicken feed!"

Then the next one goes with Piggy. It's Len. Rory points to the special candy, a big pink marshmallow.

"Come on back!" I yell.

No one comes back.

Everyone stares into the darkness.

Then Piggy comes running up, out of breath.

"Len's gone home. He got scared. He was afraid his parents would get mad, afraid of those big boys—who knows? What a ridiculous situation! I ran after him, but he was running so fast ... Who wants to go in his place?"

She's acting her part very well, I say to myself.

Everyone's quiet for a minute. Then Sam says, "I do."

"Come on, then," says Piggy. And to me she says, "Make up your mind a little bit faster."

We pick the pink marshmallow again. I say I don't think it's a good idea, but Rory says, "Shut up," so I go along with it.

"Come on back!" we all yell.

Again nothing.

"This isn't fun anymore," says Rory. "Sam, come on. Stop fooling around!"

"Piggy!" I shout. "Piggy, you hear me? Come back now!" I really want her to. I'm starting to get scared myself.

No answer from Piggy.

"Piggy!" I shout. "Piggy!"

Far in the distance Piggy says, "Yeaaah!"

"Sam?" calls Rory.

"Noooo!" says the voice of Piggy in the darkness.

"I'm going home," says one of the remaining boys.

"Me, too," says the other. They both run away.

Rory stays where he is, the only one left. "Sam?" he calls again.

Piggy steps out of the darkness. "Sam," she pants, "Sam thought he heard the city boys and he ran off right away. He thinks we've attracted their attention by shouting so loud."

Piggy grabs Rory. "Now you're the only one left. Two against one."

"I'm not scared," says Rory.

"Good," says Piggy, "'cause I know a game that's even more fun. Come on."

She pulls him into the darkness. He tries to struggle free, but Piggy has him in her iron grip.

I know that grip. I walk behind them.

My legs are moving. I can feel it. And I'm breathing faster than normal. But I don't belong here. This is something between Rory and Piggy.

Actually between Piggy and Rory.

"You open the lock, Dizzy," says Piggy when we get to the tunnel. She gives me the key. She's still got a good hold on Rory.

"What is this?" he shouts. He tries to wrestle free. Piggy pinches even harder. She's incredibly strong. "What kind of horse-shit joke is this?"

My hands are trembling. *We'll let you go right away*, I say to myself. *This is only to scare you a little*. But I don't say anything. Piggy clearly told me that we shouldn't calm them down before they get really scared. Otherwise it's all pointless. I pinch my lips together.

The lock is open. Piggy shoves Rory inside and clicks the lock shut.

"Let me out!" says Rory. He hammers on the grate.

"Why?" asks Piggy.

She laughs out loud when she sees how startled Rory is to suddenly find Sam and Len standing next to him.

"What is this, Trojan horse?" shouts Rory, his voice breaking. His voice isn't as deep as it usually is.

"Watch your language, sonny," says Piggy. "Or I'll throw away the key and you'll stay locked up here forever. My name is Piggy, not Margaret and not horsey and definitely not Trojan horse. Before I let you out, will you swear that you'll never say that again?"

"Horsey Margaret," says Rory. He spits at Piggy, but it doesn't go far enough.

"'Horsey Margaret'? Okay," says Piggy slowly. "You asked for it." She throws the key away. We hear it land somewhere in the darkness.

I know that this is what we agreed to. Piggy would pretend to throw away the key. But I could swear she really did it. She sure can act!

"Come on, Dizzy," says Piggy. "Let's go."

Rory, Sam, and Len start screaming "Let us out" at the top of their lungs. They pull on the lock. I can't stand it.

"If we bump into those drunken guys, we'll ask if they want to keep you company," says Piggy.

We turn around and walk away.

"Weren't you both going to sleep at your house?" asks my mother when we come in. Piggy's dragged me here. I can't think straight anymore.

"We were already in bed, but Dizzy wanted to come home," says Piggy.

My mother looks doubtful, but she nods. "Something to drink?" she asks. She's already walking to the kitchen to get some drinks.

In the hall there's a bicycle turned upside down.

"What are you doing?" I ask.

"I'm tinkering with that bike. When I'm done it'll spin like a top."

My mother is standing there with the orangeade in her hands.

My head is clearing up bit by bit. *Great, we'll have a quick drink and then go back and let them out,* I say to myself.

"Piggy drinks Coke," I say.

"Okay," says my mother. "Coke it is." She pours a glass of Coke.

"It makes you sleep better," says Piggy as she walks into the kitchen. She flashes her white teeth in a big smile.

"Ma'am, would it be okay if I slept here tonight?" she asks.

"Fine with me," says my mother. "But is it all right with your father?"

Sleep? I say to myself. This wasn't part of the plan. I only like to sleep by myself. There were a few times that I had to sleep in the same room with my mother, when I was sick or on vacation, and I hated it. I can't sleep if I can hear someone else move or yawn or breathe.

"Sure," says Piggy. "My father thought it was such a shame that our pajama party turned out the way it did. He knows I was going to ask him, so if I don't go home he won't be upset."

She swallows the Coke in one long gulp and pushes the glass toward the bottle. My mother pours another half a glass. Piggy tosses it back and stands up.

"You ready?" she asks. "I'd really like to go over my lines with you, and it's getting late."

I walk to the hall, to where our jackets are hanging.

My mother walks with me. "What are you going to do? You're not going outside, I hope?"

"We have to go out for just a minute," I tell her.

"No way!" says my mother. "You two are staying right here. It's already past eleven! And I'm hearing all these stories again about those drunken boys."

Piggy quickly hangs up her jacket. "Of course, ma'am," she says. "I didn't think it was a good idea, either."

We go to my room.

Piggy yawns. We pull the guest bed out from under my bed.

Piggy stretches lazily and lies down.

"Why are you afraid that someone will be able to read your mind?" she asks.

I've just started taking off my shoes and I stand still with one shoe in my hand.

"You can tell everything to your best friend, your blood sister. Everything," she says. "Is your mind that sick?"

I drop the shoe and look at her. "Would you like it if I knew exactly what you were thinking?" I ask.

Piggy shakes her head. And she doesn't laugh, fortunately.

I put on my pajamas, go to the bathroom, and close the curtains, and by the time I lie down in bed, a bundle of nerves, Piggy's already asleep.

I look at her eyelids. They're moving quickly. Her breathing is also quick, but regular. She's really sleeping.

How can she sleep at a time like this? I wake her up. "We've got to let them out," I tell her.

"Your mother won't let us go out," she says with a thick, drowsy voice. "You don't want to do something that's not allowed, do you?"

"But ...," I start.

She turns over.

"Tomorrow," she says. "Tomorrow."

She's sleeping again. But I can't sleep. I keep thinking about Rory, Sam, and Len. There in the tunnel, cold, quiet, and scared. Locked up. Their parents worried.

The floor thunders *now*, the windows sing *now*, my bed screams *now*. I think *now*. Power surges through my body.

I wake her up again. "Give me the key," I tell her. "*Now*."

"I threw it away," she says.

"Now," I say. "Hand it over."

"It's somewhere out there in the dark. You won't find it now. Maybe tomorrow. Maybe never. But not now for sure."

13

I put on my socks and my pants. And a warm sweater.

The stairs creak. I keep walking.

For the first time ever I'm happy our house is so old and that everything creaks. Then it's not so quiet. I'm not so alone.

Piggy is sound asleep. She didn't wake up when I got out of bed.

My mother is sound asleep, too. I can hear her slow breathing from under the blankets. I listen and it calms me down, as if she were talking to me in her sleep.

I have to wake her up now, I say to myself. *Tell her everything, tell the whole truth.*

Mom, I have to say, Piggy and I have locked up the kids from the square. And Mom, I want to let them out.

Then she can help me make everything better again. Let the kids go, call the parents. My mother won't be angry for long.

The room spins before my eyes. I blink.

I sit on the edge of the bed and look at my mother's sleeping face. Her tangled hair, her freckles. Her long, long eyelashes. I want to smell her warm neck, but I won't let myself do it.

"Mom," I say softly. "Mom."

My mother stirs a little. When she sees me, she smiles.

"Hello, sweetie," she says and turns toward me.

"Mom," I say, a little louder, "I did something wrong."

"We'll take care of it," my mother says, half-asleep. "Tomorrow."

I hear her breathing slow down again. Her mouth makes a very soft smacking sound.

I ought to wake her up. I ought to turn on the light and talk to her out loud so she wakes up and stays awake. She has to help me, and the boys. Now.

I pause to think.

We haven't got a key.

Hooker's shop is closed. The grate is locked.

Tomorrow my mother has to get up very early again.

Will those five hours make any difference?

Can we really do anything now?

Those boys probably went back to the city a long time ago.

And it's probably impossible to find the key in the pitch-dark.

I walk back to my room.

What will Piggy say? Actually I know for sure that she'll be angry.

I walk back to my bed. Take off my warm sweater, my pants, and my socks. Lie down. Sigh.

A few hours later I get up again. I go downstairs, to the kitchen. Boil some water and make a cup of tea. My mother has left a note on the table.

Have a good day it says.

She has to leave early every morning. That way she can work as long as possible and still be home in time, for me. Maybe the parents of Rory and Sam and Len are sitting in their kitchens, too. Maybe they haven't slept all night. What am I supposed to say to them later on, after we've let them out? I'm sorry?

That's pathetic.

Maybe they'll attack us. Maybe there'll be a fight. I don't like quarrels. I carefully take a sip of hot tea. I look outside.

It's still dark.

Too dark.

I go to school, to Nelly. The school is still locked. Everything is still quiet and dark.

I wait. When Nelly arrives, she's not surprised to see me. "Hey, it's Dizzy," she says happily. "You come to practice your catching?"

I nod. She opens the door. She starts in on the trampoline.

"Okay," I say and start getting myself ready.

Nelly stands opposite me.

She throws. Flub. The ball falls.

"Again," she says.

She throws. Another flub.

"Keep on trying," says Nelly. She throws again, and another flub.

The same thing, ten times. "Come on, Dizzy!" says Nelly. She throws, again, and again. And then—yes! I catch it.

Clumsy, but I catch it. Suddenly. The ball is in my hands.

It makes me so happy.

But sad, too.

Sam. Len. Rory.

And Piggy.

I run out of the gym.

"Dizzy? Dizzy!" calls Nelly. But I keep on running.

At home Piggy has just woken up. She doesn't ask any questions.

We walk to the tunnel. Piggy is fast, as usual, and I tag along behind.

How can I look them in the eyes? What am I supposed to say? Can I ever make it up to them? If they were to hate me for the rest of my life, I'd understand.

"Come on!" screams Piggy. "You were the one who wanted to let them out yesterday. What's keeping you?"

I keep walking. I feel like I'm going to throw up.

There they are, Rory, Len, and Sam. They're sitting all huddled together. They're cold. Sam can't stop shivering. Rory is paler than usual. He has dark rings under his eyes. His neck has completely disappeared between his hunched-up shoulders. Len has a wet spot on his pants.

I don't know where to look.

"And have the drunks dropped in to see you?" Piggy asks with a laugh, standing in front of the grate. "Have they come to piss on you yet?"

Sam is crying. "Let us out," he says.

"See? They did come back to get us out. I kept telling you they wouldn't let us starve." It's Rory's deep voice.

We look for the key. We stand just about where we were standing yesterday when Piggy threw the key away. Piggy looks in her pocket, pulls something out, bends over, and straightens up with the key in her hand.

"Ta-da!" she says.

That's impossible, I say to myself.

She *didn't* throw the key away. She had it in her pocket all night long!

"Joke!" she says to me. Something starts boiling in the pit of my stomach. This can't be true.

Sam stands up wearily. His legs are shaking. He looks to Rory for support. His face is wet and black.

Just before Piggy puts the key in the lock, she says to Rory, "You have to promise you won't say *Margaret* or *horsey* or *Trojan horse*."

Sam cries even louder.

"Let them out right now!" I hear myself scream.

"What did you say?" asks Piggy.

I scream it again.

With a strange smile on her lips she throws the key away, as far as she can.

"Do it yourself," she says.

I run to the place where I think the key has landed. As I run I say to myself: *She's mean. Really mean. Why didn't I see that before? She's never told me anything about having other girlfriends. Did she ever have any? And she plays awful piano on purpose.*

I kneel down and look in every nook and cranny.

"You have to help us!" yells Rory. "Dizzy! Dizzy!"

It's like a cheer. Sometimes they yell like this at football games. Sam and Len join in. "Diz-zy! Diz-zy!"

The key is nowhere to be found. Maybe it's a little farther to the right. Or to the left. Or farther up there, or back here. The world is spinning. Keep steady. Focus on one spot.

Piggy walks toward me. Her big shoes stop right in front of my hands. "Dizzy, you're not going to let them out, are you?" she asks very quietly. "It's 'you and me' and not 'you and them,' isn't it?"

My hands are trembling. "Dizzy!" the boys yell.

"We're blood sisters," she says, putting her shoe on my hand. *There'll be a bruise there*, I say to myself.

"Don't do it," she says. "I don't want you to. Let's go. Then we'll think up a new plan."

I keep looking at the ground. Now I have to be strong. Clear. Very, very clear. But can I?

Suddenly I think of Nelly.

Try, says Nelly. *Everything begins with trying. With practice. Succeeding isn't the important thing—it's doing.* And she's right. I'm going to catch the ball. I can do it.

The boys are counting on me.

"I've got to let them out," I say. "This is wrong—what we've done."

She bursts out in a cold laugh. She grabs my head. "So you're turning your back on me? Just like that? You're not my friend anymore? Our friendship is over, then. I don't mean anything to you. No more than a fly." She digs her shoe deeper into my hand, pressing one of her hands into my face.

I can't breathe. I push her away.

"You wanted this! You did it!" shrieks Piggy. "It's all your fault. You wanted to teach those creeps a lesson once and for all. I'm going to put all the blame on you. You can count on it."

Piggy looks me in the eyes. I try to look above her. But she looks so strange that I *have* to look at her. She's a balloon with curls. A balloon made of steel.

14

Mr. Hooker's shop isn't open yet, but he lives above the shop and I ring his doorbell. After a few minutes I hear someone bumping around.

"Hello?" shouts Mr. Hooker from an upstairs window.

"Hello, Mr. Hooker. It's me, Dizzy!" I shout back. My voice cracks a little.

"Yes?" says Mr. Hooker.

"I ... I'd like to borrow your hacksaw again. It's an emergency!"

Mr. Hooker comes slowly down the stairs. "What's going on?" he says, a little breathless. "What's the emergency?"

"Well," I say, and then I remember what he said to me before: *if you use it to do something you're not supposed to, don't tell me!*

"I can't tell you," I say quickly.

Mr. Hooker gives me a severe look. "I don't like this, Lizzy. No jokes now. I'm too old for that. What do you want to do with the saw?"

"I ... I can't really tell you," I say. My face slowly turns red.

"Just try," he says quietly.

"Yesterday we locked up three boys," I blurt out. "They've

been there all night and their parents are really worried, of course, and the boys don't look so great. ... I have to let them out, but the gate is locked and Piggy threw away the key ... so I need the hacksaw to ..."

Mr. Hooker looks me in the eyes. I don't want him to. But I *have* to keep looking at him. *He doesn't believe me!* I say to myself. And I understand that. If I hadn't done it myself, hadn't gone through it myself, I probably wouldn't believe it either.

I bow my head. "I really need the hacksaw," I say miserably.

"It's just that I've known you your whole life. ..." Mr. Hooker puts the hacksaw in my hand. "Bring it back, okay?" he says.

"As soon as I'm done!" I say and run away. *Fast, run fast,* I say to myself.

Now I can make up for everything. We can forgive and forget it all.

At the tunnel I take a good look around. I'm looking for Piggy. She's nowhere to be seen.

"Okay," says Rory. "Great. Finally somebody's acting normal!"

I start sawing with the hacksaw.

"Faster!" says Rory. "Come on!"

I saw as fast as I can. But it's slow going.

The saw keeps slipping. I keep looking around.

"She's not there," says Rory quickly. "Keep your mind on what you're doing. You have to get us out of here. Who knows when she's coming back."

I put the hacksaw back in the lock.

I start sawing. I saw with my eyes shut, my jaw shut, my mouth shut, and then, just as I'm about to give up—bingo! The lock gives way.

I quickly open the lock and pull away the chain. I open the grate.

All three step out into the light with squinting eyes. Sam and Len run off right away.

"She's crazy," says Rory, before running away himself. "She's totally nuts."

15

I run without catching my breath. I run and run. As soon as I get home I call my mother.

"Mom," I say and start to cry, "you have to come home! Now!"

"What's the matter?" says my mother. "Something was going on last night, too, wasn't there?"

"I'm so scared," I say with a shrieking howl.

She lets me cry myself out. She says quiet, kind words to me. Once I'm a little calmer, I tell her what happened.

I talk. I cry. I whisper. At the end of my story my mother doesn't say anything for a long, long time.

"Unbelievable," she finally says.

And, luckily very quietly, "I'm coming. You know it could take a while, but I'm coming. Now."

The doorbell rings. The noise is loud and long, and it cuts through the silence.

Don't open the door, I say to myself.

The ringing stops and starts again right away.

"Don't pay any attention," I say aloud in the empty house.

I go upstairs.

The ringing doesn't stop.

I go into my room.

I sit on my bed. Crawl under the covers.

The ringing doesn't stop.

I stand up and shut the curtains.

"You're home," I hear Rory's father call. "I know you're home!"

I put my hands over my ears.

"Hello!" he cries again. "Dizzy! Dizzy! Open the door! I have to talk to you!"

I'm sitting motionless on my bed.

"The others have already gone to the police, but I want to talk to you first!"

I can wait, I say to myself. *I can do that.*

Now I have to wait. Until Mom's here. When she's here, everything will be all right.

But another voice in me says everything won't be all right. How can this ever be all right? The boys went home and told their parents everything. They went to the police. Now Rory's father wants to talk to me. He wants me to explain it all. But there's nothing to explain.

Only that Piggy is my friend, *was* my friend, and that we were going to carry out her plan. But Piggy will say it was *my* plan. It's her word against mine. And she talks more, better, louder than I do. They'll believe her and hate me.

He keeps ringing the bell. Nonstop.

I sit on my bed under the covers and cover my ears.

I'm not here. I don't want to be here.

What can I think about? I pinch my eyes shut even tighter. Then I see Piggy.

She's looking at me with angry eyes.

I open my eyes again. My cheeks are wet with tears.

I have to keep my eyes open, I say to myself. *It's much worse with my eyes closed.*

"Dizzy!" calls Rory's father outside. "Dizzy, open the door!"

I lean against the wall and groan. My heart is beating like crazy. What am I supposed to do? Is there any way out?

16

"Lizzy? Lizzy! What's the matter?"

There's a hand on my shoulder. I slap it angrily.

It's Dykstra. She looks worried.

"I have to go to the bathroom," I tell her.

I've been pretending that I didn't notice her hand. I just kept on going. Kept on going.

But now it doesn't help. I have to stop.

The clock behind me is ticking the time away. I have to stop talking.

There's pressure at the bottom of my stomach. It hurts. It stings. When I take a deep breath I feel like I'm about to explode.

"I really have to go," I tell her.

It smells like sweat in the hall. Sweat and cigarette smoke. Dykstra walks right next to me. She grabs my upper arm for a minute.

I pull my arm away. That's just where it hurts. Dykstra sees my black-and-blue bruises.

"Did I do that?" she asks, startled.

I really want to say yes, but I say no.

"Who did?" she asks.

I don't say anything.

She whistles through her teeth. Frowns. "That's pretty bad," she says.

"Is she here yet?" I ask.

She stops at the bathroom door.

"Go ahead," she says. "I'll wait in the hall."

When I'm done I wash my hands at the little sink. It's really too small. Lots of water ends up on the gray-green floor.

Am I talking too much? I wonder.

We walk back through the stuffy hall. In another room I can hear muffled screaming, the sound of rushing, panic. We go back into the interrogation room.

"We have to continue," says Dykstra. Her eyes are watery. "Your mother said that locking the boys up in the tunnel was a kind of joke. But it didn't stop and then it wasn't funny anymore. The boys were really scared in the tunnel." She looks up and tries to look past me. "Do you understand that? They were really scared."

"So was I," I say. "Rory's father was screaming so loud. I was all huddled up, waiting for my mother to come."

I look at the wall. "Can I tell you exactly what happened?"

"Please do," says Dykstra.

•

My mother says, "We're going to Piggy's house. She has to explain why this happened. And her father has to know, too. He doesn't know what she's been up to. He's always so busy with his work."

Rory's father laughs. It's a strange laugh. "Have you ever seen her father?" he asks. "He doesn't work. He spends every day at Up in the Clouds. He's there when they open their doors. Totally lost his way. He and his daughter never talk to each other. The father leaves home every morning, pretending he's going to work. And she pretends to believe him. It's really pathetic."

"It's not true!" I say. "Her father works for the government. Secret work." I still remember very clearly what she told me at her house when she was sitting at the piano. She played a happy song the whole time. After that I wasn't allowed to go home. I had to help her go over her lines.

Rory's father shakes his head. "It's sad," he says. "They have to keep moving because of that kid of his. He hates all that moving. It's getting the better of him."

"Why do they have to keep moving?" I ask. "What does she do?" But I really don't want to hear the answer.

"Hard to imagine a stunt that kid hasn't pulled: disturbing the peace, extortion, shoplifting, violence ... She just keeps it up. Then they have a fight with the whole neighborhood. And then they move."

My mother grabs me firmly by the elbow. "Let's go."

All the windows of the white house are open. The curtains are wide open, too. We can look right inside. Piggy sees us coming. The door swings open. And there she is, smiling.

"Well, what do you know," she says. "Visitors." She has a bottle of Coke in her hand.

"We didn't come to chat," says Rory's father right away. "You little bitch!"

"Little bitch?"

"Do you have any idea how worried we were?" he asks. And he says it again, only angrier: "Do you have any idea how worried we were?"

Piggy laughs. She just laughs at him!

"Don't you laugh!" says Rory's father with a threatening voice.

"Joke," she says.

Rory's father takes a step forward. Now he's right in front of her nose. She's bigger than he is.

"You know what I think is a joke?" he asks her.

She keeps laughing.

"You ... you ... dirty little ..." He shoots forward and grabs her by the throat.

My mother pulls on his arm, panic-stricken. He lets Piggy go.

"Oooo," says Piggy slowly. "You're not supposed to do that. That's against the law. I think I may have to report it. Assault."

"And what do you think I'm going to report? Abduction and confinement!"

"And I hope for your sake that they lock her up for a long time," says Piggy, and she looks at me.

My face gets red. Rory's father is about to fly at her. My mother is barely able to restrain him.

"It was her idea!" says Piggy. "Look, I don't care what

happens in this two-bit town. I'm out of here soon anyway. We're moving again. But she ..." She points to me. "*She's* been teased and humiliated and ignored for years and she finally saw her chance to get even. I didn't want to. I thought it was going too far. Way too far. But she begged me. She *begged* me! I figured this was her chance. Her only chance."

"It's not true!" I shout.

Piggy takes a swallow of Coke from the bottle in her hand and keeps on talking, as if I hadn't said anything. "And now you all come to my house. You think I'm the guilty one. Because I don't come from here, of course. Well, it's all *her* fault that this happened. I just went along with it. She's the one who's guilty. It's her."

"You little wretch," says my mother. "I thought you were friends."

"Who wants to be friends with her?" Piggy waves her hand dismissively.

"We're going," says my mother coldly.

I walk with her. I look back. And there's Piggy. Standing stock-still. Alone.

She raises her hand. She winks. Piggy winks! Almost automatically I start walking back.

I take three steps, four. Then I stop and turn around.

"And that's what happened," I say to Dykstra. I look around the office. "Can I go now? You know all there is to know."

"Why did you do it?" asks Dykstra. "Why didn't you warn anybody?"

I take a deep breath. Dykstra is sitting across from me. She picks up a pen without looking. Chews on the end. The table between us is not tidy. It's messy. But she knows where everything is.

Dykstra looks at me. I look back. Just for a minute.

"I don't know."

There's a lot of noise behind the door. Tables are being shoved around roughly, a chair falls over.

"I didn't like it," I say. "She did."

More noise from behind the door.

People are walking back and forth. Doors slam. Shouts.

The door swings open.

Dirks steps into the interrogation room. "Something terrible has happened!" he says.

It's Piggy, I know right away.

And yet I ask, "Is it Piggy?"

Dirks nods. He clears his throat.

Suddenly I can see Piggy before me, in the hospital, covered with blood. "Is it serious?" I ask.

Dirks nods.

Piggy, in the hospital. Someone pulls a sheet up over her face. I sniffle loudly.

"Margaret stabbed the drama teacher in his stomach this morning with a strange knife. A dagger," says Dirks. He looks at me. "The teacher is in the hospital. He's in critical condition. Margaret has been brought here. She's just come in."

I feel myself falling into a deep black hole. And I hear myself sliding across the floor, like a sack of flour going down the stairs.

17

"Lizzy! Lizzy!"

I blink.

"Honey," says my mother. She takes me in her arms. I smell the delicious warm smell of her neck.

"You okay?" Dirks asks.

"Sort of," I say truthfully.

"Here's some water," says my mother. She lets me go. "I'll have some, too. I'm shaking like a leaf. I heard it on the local radio station and I came here right away. It's unbelievable. And with your dagger ... At least, that's what the people here think. ..."

My dagger ...

I give her the dagger. She carefully runs her finger along the flat sides.

"It's very sharp," I say. But then I see she's already cut herself. There's a tiny bit of blood on the edge of the knife. She runs her finger along the sharp edge once again and it bleeds even harder.

"You're bleeding," I say.

"I see that," says Piggy calmly. She just keeps it up, running her finger along the sharp edge without blinking an eye. "It's so sharp you can't even feel it." She looks dreamily at her bleeding finger.

•

"Lizzy, honey," says my mother. "Can you hear me?"

I take a sip of water.

"It was just before first period. The cafeteria was packed," says Dirks. "The drama teacher was having a cup of coffee with a couple of students, as usual. He likes that more than staying in the teachers' room. Margaret came into the cafeteria holding that strange wavy knife in front of her and just stabbed him in the stomach. It happened so fast that no one could stop her."

"She had problems with that teacher," I say.

"But that's no reason to stab someone!" cries my mother.

"No," I say. "Of course not."

"The teacher collapsed," Dirks goes on. "Fortunately the janitor kept his head. He grabbed Margaret and asked the cafeteria lady to call 911. I went to pick her up myself. She's my responsibility because of the other matter." He sighs. "The teacher is in intensive care. He's in pretty bad shape. They haven't spoken with him yet. He's on a respirator. But even if he had been able to talk, he'd be too weak."

No one says anything. The clock is ticking.

"The teacher has a wife and two young children," says my mother. "That's what they said on the radio."

I don't want to be here. I don't want to hear this.

I listen to the clock.

The ticking sounds loud in the small room. Twenty-one, twenty-two, twenty-three.

"To think that she did it with your dagger ..." My mother's voice fades into the distance.

"At least that's what we think," says Dykstra.

"We still have to check it out," Dirks adds.

My mother nods. "Somebody's already looking into it. I gave them my key. Piggy must have taken the dagger the night she slept at our house. She must have known already that she was going to do it."

"Maybe," says Dirks.

"Everybody says, 'I could kill you' some time or another," my mother says. "But she actually did it!"

The room is spinning.

"She didn't put up a fight. She just came along with me," says Dirks. "I'm going to talk to her now." He turns around. When he gets to the doorway he stops, with his back to me. "You know what was so weird? She was in a cafeteria full of people, the janitor was holding on to her, but it was as if she was completely alone. Completely alone. She looked down at the floor and she didn't say anything. Didn't do anything. Her arms were just hanging loose. A pathetic fat girl. You couldn't imagine that she had just stabbed someone."

I swallow. There's something heavy in my throat.

Dirks keeps on walking.

I swallow, but the feeling in my throat doesn't go away.

18

We're standing outside, my mother and I. It's raining. She hurries to the car, walking ahead of me.

Someone's coming toward us. There's a camera hanging around his neck.

"Hurry up," says my mother. "Keep on walking." She tries to open the car door but she drops the key.

The man with the camera calls, "Can I ask you some questions? Are you the friend of that girl who just stabbed the teacher?"

My mother has picked up the key and is sticking it in the lock. "Get lost," she hisses.

We get in and she drives away, tires screeching.

The streets are gleaming in the rain. The windows of the car get all steamed up. I pick up the chamois and wipe the windows, stretching to get the back windows as clean as I can.

We drive through the busy streets. It's quiet in the car. Neither one of us says anything. My mother is biting her lower lip.

"How do you feel now?" she finally asks.

I shake my head. *As if I've been anesthetized,* I say to

myself. *I don't feel anything. Or as if there's a big, thick down blanket over me, keeping everything out.*

"I don't know," I say. "I wish I were out on the field, at my favorite spot."

We have to stop for a traffic light. A bicyclist wobbles next to our car. He rests his hand on the roof. I duck down. Not my head, don't touch my head.

My mother takes a roll of candy out of the glove compartment. She hands it to me. They're the kind of candies you suck on. For a long time. I give two to my mother and take two myself.

The light turns green. My mother steps on the gas.

We drive on. Two-lane roads. Three-lane roads. Two-lane roads. One-lane road. It stops raining. The familiar shapes of our neighborhood fill the windows. Our town. The church. The square. The supermarket.

My mother stops to let the bus go first, the bus that comes only once an hour in the evening.

"Mom," I say, "I want to get out!"

She nods. "Fine. You want to have a little walk, right?"

I get out, shut the car door, and walk to the bus stop. I lean against the pole and wait.

I stand. I look. I lean. For a long time.

NOW

That was a year ago, and now Piggy sent me that letter.

Dear Dizzy,

How are you?

The people here wanted me to leave you alone for at least a year. So I did.

They said to me, if this is still on your mind after a year, you'll be allowed to write her a letter.

This is that letter.

What's still on my mind is that I really want to see you again.

How about coming to see me sometime? I'd really like that, blood sister.

There, I said it.

Anxiously waiting to see if you write back—or better, if you come see me.

Yours, Piggy.

"Why?" asked my mother. "Why did she have to send you this letter? Now that you're doing so well!"

I thought about it. Was I doing well? I didn't know. I really didn't know. Are you doing well if you still wake up with a start every night? Are you doing well if you think about it every day?

Fortunately the teacher survived. After two weeks he came out of the coma. No brain damage. But he's never going to teach again.

Piggy didn't say anything. Absolutely nothing. She stopped talking altogether.

And me ... Well, it was never as bad as it was at first. Never so open and painful. But it wasn't over. Everything had changed, for good.

"I don't know if I'm doing well," I said.

"I think you are," said my mother. "I think you understand things better now."

I nodded. That was probably true. At Evergreen Hills they said the same thing. *More insight*—that was in my last report card.

Other things have changed, too. I've noticed that I'm better at "standing up to things." Better at saying *period* after I've said what's on my mind. Now I know that other people can't just guess what I'm thinking. They can't see inside my head.

I don't get nervous so quickly, either. You know why? It's almost impossible for anything worse to happen than what happened back then. And if it does, I now know that the day it happens will fade further and further into the past. Time is on your side. You may not realize it—at first you don't think so. But it happens anyway.

And then there's that time with Rory. One week after it

all happened, Rory came up to me. I was leaning against the lamppost. He stood in front of me and looked at me. I looked over his head. He pushed the ball into my hands.

"Dizzy is it," he said to the others. I stood in the middle. Rory stood right in front of me and said softly with his deep voice, "Just throw."

I stood there with the ball and didn't do anything.

Slowly and softly Rory said, "Throw, Dizzy!" Sam and Len joined in: "Throw, Dizzy!"

I threw the ball—and hit him. I hit him!

Then Rory went to stand in the middle and he hit Len. I joined in. It only happened once, but even so ...

Sometimes they're grouchy and annoying, and then they call me "retard." But sometimes they call Rory "corpse" because he's always so pale.

"I'm going back to the shop," said my mother. "But drop in if you want."

I nodded.

"Will you do that, honey?" said my mother.

I nodded. "I'll come by."

Mr. Hooker died last year. In his sleep. One day his shop didn't open. People thought it was strange. They rang the doorbell and he didn't answer. He was lying in bed. Dead.

My mother bought his shop. I didn't know she wanted to do anything like that, but she's really happy with her own business. It's close to home and I can drop in as much as I want. And I do.

The business is running pretty well. She's made a lot of changes and everything's been painted in bright colors. She was able to rent the apartment over the shop to a childless couple. And I got a brand-new bike.

My mother stopped at the doorway and turned around.

"Are you going?" she asked.

"What?" I said.

"Are you going to visit her?"

"We were friends," I said indecisively. "Sort of friends."

"Really?" asked my mother. "Did you like being her friend?"

"No. It wasn't much fun. Mostly not."

I thought a minute.

Why should I go? What was I supposed to say?

"I'm not going," I said to my mother. "Period."